Star-Crossed

Cal's Story

AMBER D. LEWIS

Print Paperback ISBN: 978-1-7370541-8-4

Ebook ISBN: 978-1-7370541-9-1

Cover Design and Formatting: Once Upon an Amber Dawn

Cover Art: Amber D. Lewis and Benjamin Lewis

Editor: Andi L. Gregory

For Business Inquiries visit www.amberdlewis.com or write to 4359 Wade Hampton Blvd, #282, Taylors, SC 29687

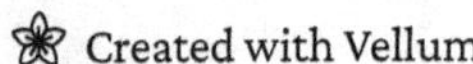 Created with Vellum

To everyone who deserves to find love and be loved. Yes, that's you, dear reader.

ALSO BY AMBER D. LEWIS
RECOMMENDED READING ORDER

THE NIGHT THE STARS FELL

SCARS: ALAK'S STORY

THE STARLIGHT IN THE SHADOWS

STAR-CROSSED: CAL'S STORY

AUTHOR NOTE

This story contains negative comments and views against the LGBTQIA+ community as displayed by fictional characters. These views are not reflected by the author. The main character also expresses self-doubt and struggles with his sexuality, especially after a forced outing occurs. Throughout the book he learns to accept himself and has the support of multiple friends.

This story also alludes to an eating disorder as well as bouts of anxiety and depression.

For more information please visit the author's website: www.amberdlewis.com/content-warnings

ONE

A dvance!" Captain Bramfield—Bram—barks.

Without hesitation, we charge forward against our opponents, swords clashing. I meet Noah blow for blow, striking fast and sure.

"Withdraw!" Bram shouts, and we break apart.

I grin at Noah as I wipe sweat from my brow with the back of my arm. He returns the grin, but we're careful not to let Bram catch us. Heaven forbid we have any fun during our morning training session. I glance over to Bram, but his eyes aren't on me. They aren't on any of the Guard. He's watching soldiers training a field over, curiosity gleaming in his eyes. After a moment, he snaps his focus back to us and we all straighten to attention.

"Good work, men," he says with a nod of satisfaction. "There is a reason you are all members of Prince Ehren's Guard, but you need to stay sharp. Dismissed."

We fall into a bustle of chatter as we sheathe swords and swagger off the training field. I'm sauntering away with everyone else when Bram draws my attention.

"Cal, Noah, come here for a minute."

I exchange a curious glance with Noah, but he shrugs as we make our way over to Bram.

"When was the last time either of you took a look at the newer recruits wanting to be part of Ehren's Guard?" Bram asks, his eyes drifting back over to the soldiers training nearby.

"I'm not sure. I think last week sometime," I reply with a shrug.

"Same here," Noah agrees with a nod. "Sometime last week."

Bram looks back at us and nods. "Would you mind checking them out again? I heard there were quite a few new soldiers, several of whom who have expressed interest in the Guard. See if there is anyone we should keep an eye on."

"No problem, Captain." I grin.

"Very good," Bram says. "You may go."

Without another word Bram turns and strides away. Noah looks over at me and bursts out laughing.

"What?" I ask, eyes sparkling.

"Do you think Bram ever has any fun, or does he think about swords night and day?" Noah asks, walking toward the nearby training field.

I grin as I fall into step beside him. "I have no idea. In all the years I've known him, he always seems so serious."

"He needs a girl something awful."

I duck my head and will away the blush that always rises when the other soldiers start talking about girls. I'm not embarrassed by any rowdy talk, but I always feel at a loss with what I can contribute. Girls have never held any interest for me, and the fewer people that know about that, the better. I'm relieved when we reach the edge of the training field and I'm no longer expected to reply.

"I don't see many new faces," Noah mutters, squinting at the sweaty soldiers.

I let my eyes wander over the gathered men. "Me neither. Maybe the newer recruits are training somewhere else or at a different time?"

Noah nods and cracks his neck. "Well, since there's nothing for me to do here, I think I'm going to head into the city. Care to join me?"

I'm about to agree when one of the soldiers catches my eye. He's young, likely a year or two younger than my age of nineteen, with a head full of shaggy, loose blond curls made brighter by his tanned skin. Even from this distance I catch the bright flash of his smile, and I can't look away.

"Cal?" Noah says, waving his hand in front of my face.

I blink, shifting my gaze to him. "Sorry, I think I'm going to hang around here for a bit more. See if any more soldiers join. I might even head over to one of the other training fields and look for those new recruits."

Noah shrugs. "Whatever suits your fancy. I guess I'll catch up with you later."

He bounds off and I turn my attention back to the sparring soldiers. They're rearranging into organized lines now, so it takes me a moment to find the young man again. When I do, I'm mesmerized by his every movement. He has skill, that's undeniable, but even I know he falls short of the requirement for the Guard. Pity. I wouldn't mind training by his side every day. As if he could hear my thoughts, the young man looks up, his bright eyes meeting mine. My face flushes with sudden shame. The man grins, nearly getting hit by the sword of his opponent. I quickly pull my gaze away and rush from the field. The last thing I need is him asking me questions. I need to disappear. Now.

THE NEXT FEW days are busy. Ehren has a short trip planned next week, and several of us will be escorting him. Bram wants to make sure we're all ready to go and has us participating in extra drill sessions. I don't have the heart to tell him a few more hours of practice a day won't make that much of a difference. The poor fellow seems to live to swing that sword of his. After one particularly brutal training session, Bram pulls me aside.

"Would you mind being part of the detail tomorrow?" he asks as I wipe the sweat from my brow.

"I wouldn't mind at all."

Bram nods. "Good." He hesitates a moment before asking, "Were you able to observe the new recruits and find anyone promising?"

I pause. I haven't been back to the training sessions since the young man caught me watching.

"There is one newer soldier who might have potential," I say, stretching the truth but only barely.

Bram nods with satisfaction. "Good to hear. There are a few soldiers attempting the trials today. I am headed over there now. Would you like to come with me, see if any of the soldiers you spotted are among those trying out?"

I freeze. Do I want to see the young man again? Yes. Do I want to run the risk of him recognizing me? No. Then again, what are the chances that he's actually among the few longing to be part of the Guard?

"I know Ehren appreciates any and all input. He trusts your opinion, as do I."

And then there's Ehren. I'm sure it's as cliché as can be to have a crush on the crown prince, but it's one I've harbored for nearly a decade now. As if a soldier like me could ever have a shot at the prince, even if he were interested in men. But, even if I don't remotely have a chance, I still enjoy his company and leap at every opportunity to be near him.

"I suppose I could join you," I concede with a shrug.

"Great," Bram says, clapping me on the shoulder. "Let's head on over."

Nerves twist in my gut as I follow Bram to the upper training ring where the trials take place. In order to enter specific training for Ehren's Guard, soldiers have to pass three trials, each with a different weapon and playing to different strengths. Bram leads the tests, switching up the exact weapons that will be used each time.

The trials may be difficult, but they're only half the battle. Once a candidate makes it past the trials, they integrate into the Guard, where they prove themselves clean of character, compatible with the other members of the Guard, and skilled beyond the average soldier. They have one month to be chosen. Those that make the cut get to be members of Ehren's Guard; the others join the king's army as basic foot soldiers. Sometimes Bram and Ehren decide within days, but other times it takes the full month. So far Ehren's Guard consists of thirty-six men, including Captain Bramfield and myself.

When we arrive at the upper training ring, the space outside the wall swarms with people, mostly soldiers, eager for a good show. Bram pushes through the crowd, making his way to Ehren at the front. I stick close to his side as the crowd parts. Ehren leans forward onto the tallest, chest-high portion of the wall, chin propped up on his palm as he watches the stretching soldiers with rapt attention.

I step to his side and realize with a rush of fear and excitement the young man I saw is among those trying out. He wears a cocky yet charming grin that makes my heart flutter.

"Do you see any of the soldiers that caught your eye?" Bram says in my ear, making me jump.

"Oh, uh, yes. That young man right there was one I had my eye on," I mumble, nodding toward him.

Bram scowls, looking right at the young man in question. "That one?"

It's extremely unfortunate he happens to fumble and drop a sword at that exact moment. The tips of my ears turn bright red.

"He seemed more competent before," I mutter, regretting my decision to come along.

"Cal's right," Ehren says cheerfully, eyes bright as he straightens and playfully bumps his shoulder against mine. "I was watching him when he first came up here, and he seems to have decent skill. He was the first to arrive and seems very eager."

"Eager does not equate talent," Bram says, scanning the other participants with a scowl.

Ehren shrugs, placing his palms flat against the stone to hoist himself up to sit on top of the wall. "It seems like he may have some talent, too."

Bram offers Ehren an appeasing shrug before circling around the wall to the center of the ring. Ehren turns, looking down at me with a wide grin, and motions for me to join him on the wall. I oblige as Bram whistles loudly, drawing the attention of both the crowd and the recruits.

"The process to become a Guard member is simple, but the tests are not," he says, his voice carrying easily over the open air. "They consist of three rounds, each slightly harder than the last. Anyone who can complete all three rounds will be considered for entry into training to become part of Prince Ehren's Guard. The final decision and test falls to His Majesty, Prince Ehren, and myself. Any questions?" All the contestants shake their heads. "Good. Let's begin."

Bram steps back to the side of the ring near where Ehren and I watch, motioning to one of the five young men waiting off to the side. The man stumbles forward, glancing around nervously. The first test is a simple sword fight against Pascal, a current Guard. The first contestant wins without any trouble, but fails the second test, which is hand-to-hand combat with a rather burly soldier who's part of the royal army. Next up is the young man I have my eye on. He saunters to the center of the ring with a confident swagger. At first, his form is flawless, and even Bram seems impressed. He doesn't adjust quickly enough, however, and Pascal learns to predict his moves. It's not long before he's disarmed and the round is over. He looks crestfallen as he takes his place next to the other soldier who failed.

"Pity," Ehren mumbles. "He looked promising at first."

Bram nods. "He did."

I try not to let my attention obviously wander as we watch the three remaining contestants. In the end, none of them pass all three rounds. The fact that he wasn't the only one to fail seems to make my young man brighten a bit, but I still catch the clear disappointment on his face as he shuffles away.

"Well," Ehren says with a long sigh, hopping down off the wall, "shall we go grab a pint at The Gilded Goblet to commiserate the fact that my Guard will *never* have fifty members?"

Bram rolls his eyes. "You are being dramatic. It takes time to build up a reliable Guard. It does not—and should not—happen overnight, but it will happen." He turns his attention to me. "What drew your attention to that second contestant?"

My cheeks warm as I glance away from his prying eyes. "He seemed very skilled in training compared to the other soldiers."

I expect Bram to question me further, but instead he nods. "I can definitely see his potential. He merely needs a little more focus and training. Keep an eye on him for us, will you, Cal?"

I nod, trying not to seem too eager.

"Either way, pub?" Ehren presses, waggling his eyebrows and making me laugh.

Bram and I give in and follow Ehren into the city to The Gilded Goblet. It's busy and, as much as I enjoy being in Ehren's presence, I don't care for the crowd. After one drink, I slip out, heading back toward the upper training field. I expect to find it empty and am startled when I see the young man from earlier training alone. I stand back a little, watching in awe as he trains. His muscles flex and sweat soaks his clothes, but he doesn't slow down or stop. I deeply admire his determination. When he finally stops, he sweeps his arm across his brow, glancing around. I panic when he starts to look my way, scurrying off before he can spot me, my heart thrumming against my ribcage.

TWO

A few weeks ago, Ehren, as part of his training to one day rule Callenia, was forced to attend one of his father's meetings with commoners requesting aid. A representative from the village of Bellvale brought news of flooding due to unprecedented rain and requested aid to rebuild. Ehren took special interest in the request, and the king, probably hoping to engage Ehren in leading in any way he could, put Ehren in charge of the project. Ehren took the job seriously, and when he received word that the village was rebuilt, he insisted on visiting to confirm. Many of the nobles scoffed, believing Ehren was only looking for an excuse to escape, but I know better. While I have no doubt that Ehren would indeed relish any trip away from the palace, I know how much genuine love and concern Ehren has for his people. He would not be satisfied with second-hand information. He would want to see the progress with his own two eyes. This was the mission I got to join, along with Bram and seven other Guard members.

Traveling as part of Ehren's Guard is always enjoyable,

no matter the length of the trip. This journey to the small village of Bellvale, a little way south of Embervein, takes two full days to reach. We pull into the town shortly before sunset on the second day. A man rushes up to us almost immediately.

"Your Majesty," he says with a low bow. "My name is Melvin Penbrook. We are honored to have you as our guest here in Bellvale."

"Please," Ehren says, barely masking a grimace, "there's no need to bow."

His voice is even and carefree, but I know him well enough to catch the discomfort in his voice. As long as I have known him, Ehren has wanted to be treated more like anyone else and less like a prince.

"Whatever you wish, Your Majesty," the man says, straightening. "We've set aside rooms for you and your Guard at our finest inn, if I may show you the way?"

"Please," Ehren says, gesturing for the man to lead.

"The inn is above a tavern that serves a fine stew, if that would suit you, Your Majesty," Melvin says as he walks alongside Ehren, guiding us toward the inn. "Of course, if you would prefer something else, we could always—"

"I very much like stew," Ehren cuts in with a genuine smile.

The man releases a long breath of relief at Ehren's words, noticeably relaxing. When we reach the inn, we dismount and Bram instructs two Guards to take care of our horses while the rest of us accompany Ehren inside. Bram surveys the inside of the tavern the moment we step through the door, assessing every possible threat. While it's busy, barely half the tables are full. As soon as the owner spots us, he approaches with his head bowed.

"We may need to make a few adjustments in order to secure the room for the prince," Bram says to the man before he even gets a chance to speak.

"Of course," the man says, nodding his head enthusiastically. "Whatever you need."

"We also need our room information."

"I've that all ready for ya," the man says, withdrawing a few keys from his apron pocket and extending them to Bram.

Bram accepts the keys with a nod of satisfaction before turning to me. "Cal, escort Ehren upstairs to his room and help him deposit our travel bags. Remain with him until I secure the area."

Ehren sighs dramatically and mumbles under his breath, "I don't need a damn babysitter."

Bram shoots Ehren an admonishing look as I collect the bags from the others. "You most certainly do, and you know it."

Ehren rolls his eyes, plucking the keys from Bram and throwing a couple bags over his shoulder. "Fine. Come along, Cal. Try to keep me out of trouble as we walk up a staircase and down a hall. I'm sure it's a trying job."

I bite back a grin, stumbling along behind Ehren as he strides away from Bram and up the stairs at the corner of the tavern. It takes only a moment for us to find our rooms. Ehren selects the smaller of the rooms with two beds, insisting the Guard requires larger rooms than he does. Ehren's barely inside his room before he dumps the bags on the floor. I add mine to the pile before shutting the door behind me. Ehren closes his eyes and inhales deeply, a smile on his lips as he takes in the room.

"I love this," he confesses, turning to me, eyes bright.

I quirk an eyebrow at him. "Questionable tavern rooms?"

Ehren laughs. It's a beautiful, rich sound that makes my heart beat faster. I'm suddenly very aware that I'm alone with the prince in an inn. A warm blush creeps up my neck.

"No," Ehren replies, completely oblivious to my sudden discomfort. "I love being away from the palace, being on the road. A kingdom isn't simply taxes and exports. It's the people. When I'm king, I'm not just going to sit in my comfortable palace, relying on spies and messengers. No, I'm going to travel. I'm going to check up on the actual people of my kingdom as often as I can. They won't need to come to me, because I'll be coming to them."

He speaks with such fervor I can't hide my smile. "You'll be an amazing king one day."

Ehren's face grows slightly more serious as he asks, "Do you really think so?"

I nod, taking a step toward him. "I really do. I doubt there's any prince or king who loves his people as much as you love yours."

Ehren's eyes lock with mine and my heart skips a beat. It's moments like this where I almost wonder if we could be true friends—if maybe we could even be something more. But Ehren breaks the gaze, looking around the room, and the moment is lost. I clear my throat and glance down at the bags.

"I suppose we should leave these here for now, and we'll sort them after dinner."

Ehren glances over his shoulder at me. "I suppose. That makes the most sense."

A knock on the door makes me jump. I answer it, hand on the hilt of my sword, but relax when I find Pascal.

"Captain Bramfield said it's okay to bring Ehren on down."

I nod and turn to tell Ehren, but he's already striding toward us.

"Good," Ehren says, brushing past me into the hall. "I'm starving."

I fight back a laugh and follow Ehren and Pascal downstairs. Bram has cleared the entire back corner of the tavern, setting up Guards in close proximity across the space. We're all seated close enough so we can converse, but we're spread out enough to give us room to fight if needed. Ehren settles next to Bram and motions for me to take the seat across from him.

As the food is served, everyone around me falls into easy conversation, but I feel like an outsider. Despite having trained with several of these men since childhood, I've never really connected with them. Noah is the closest I have to a true friend, but he wasn't selected for this mission. I always feel close and friendly with Ehren, despite his rank, when we're one-on-one or with Bram at times, but in a crowd like this, I feel like I'm pushing in, unwanted, though Ehren has only ever treated me as an equal. I know the barriers are all in my head, but I can never shake the feeling of loneliness that overtakes me when I'm in the middle of a crowd. Nerves swell in my stomach and I find myself unable to eat, merely poking at my stew with a spoon to give the illusion of eating so nobody notices.

We stay downstairs in the tavern for hours, drinking ale and mead once we finish our dinner. I nurse a single tankard, never quite finishing. When Ehren starts singing bar songs a little too loudly, Bram decides it's time we head upstairs.

"Do you mind sleeping in the room with Ehren?" Bram asks, his eyes scanning Ehren's room as I distribute the bags to the others.

I arch my eyebrows, panic tightening in my chest. Bram is always the one to share a room with Ehren when it's required.

"Me?"

Bram nods firmly. "Yes. I want to stay outside for a bit and secure the perimeter. We arrived too late in the day for me to do it well enough before night fell, and I want to be thorough. I will station an additional guard outside the room, but since there is an available bed it might be a good idea to have someone stationed in here as well."

I swallow and manage a nod. "I can handle that."

"Excellent," Bram says, turning and leaving the room.

"So, we're roomies tonight, eh?" Ehren grins from where he's perched on the edge of his bed.

I turn toward him, nerves making my heart race as I force a smile.

"I suppose. You don't mind, do you? Because if you do I can—"

Ehren waves me off. "Of course I don't mind. I never mind sharing a room with friends. You especially."

My eyes brighten, the tightness in my chest loosening a touch. "You think of me as a friend?"

Ehren tilts his head, eyeing me curiously. "Of course I do. We've known each other for years and trained side-by-side together. You even call me by my name without my title." His curiosity turns into a concerned frown. "Do you see *me* as a friend? Or am I merely the prince you serve?"

I take a hurried step toward Ehren, nearly tripping over my own feet. "I do consider you a friend. I have since we were boys. I just . . . You're the prince, and I'm not even a noble."

Ehren studies me for a moment, cocking his head as a grin spreads across his face. "If you were a noble, there'd be even less a chance we'd be friends."

I fight a smile of my own as I add, "I don't doubt that, but the line between your royal title and my role as your Guard could become more distinct day by day as the possibility of you becoming king grows. I'd never presume that you see me in the same friendly way that I see you, even if you saw me that way when we were children."

Ehren's grin fades back into the frown. "Do I . . . Have I made you feel less? Or unworthy?"

My ears burn red as I hurry to shake my head. "No. Never."

Ehren sighs, a relieved smile curling on his lips. "Good. I would never want anything—especially my title—to come between our friendship." I smile and Ehren's eyes shine as he adds, "Now, *friend*, can you help me get my boots off? I could normally do it, but they seem to be moving on their own."

I laugh and cross the remainder of the room, kneeling down to remove his boots. Once Ehren's boots are off, he starts removing his shirt. I jump to my feet, face red.

"Wh-what are you doing?"

Ehren scowls at me, pausing, his shirt half on, half off. "I don't usually sleep in a shirt. Is that a problem?"

I swallow and glance away, trying to steady my racing heart. "No, it's fine."

I look back up, meeting Ehren's eyes. How do I say anything without making him hate me? How do I explain that I'm attracted to him and sleeping in a room with him is difficult enough? Even with the sliver of his stomach and chest that's currently exposed, my heart thrums wildly in my chest and my mind is conjuring scenarios I have no right to consider. If Ehren knew, he'd have me removed immediately—from his room and possibly from his Guard.

"I just . . . never mind. It's fine."

Ehren pulls his shirt down, shaking his head. "No, if it makes you uncomfortable, it's not fine. I can sleep with it on. Gods, my head is pounding."

Before I can say another word, Ehren swings his legs up on the bed and snuggles under the covers. I mumble something about locking the door and securing the room as Ehren turns his back to me. I poke my head out in the hall and confirm that Bram has stationed Jasper outside the door. By the time I'm ready for bed, Ehren is fast asleep, his chest rising and falling in even succession. With a sigh of relief, I settle into my own bed and drift off.

THE NEXT MORNING, Ehren takes several minutes to wake up, but it's nothing a little coffee can't fix. Ehren guzzles down two mugs before he comes back to life, but once he's ready he's practically giddy with exploring the town. Melvin meets us outside the tavern and guides us through the village, pointing out the spots and areas that required repair, describing in detail how they used the money. Ehren nods along, not knowing what the man is saying half the time, but his encouraging smile never fades. When the tour is finished, Ehren turns to the man.

"So, what additional funds do you require?"

The man blinks rapidly. "Additional funds?"

"Yes," Ehren replies, crossing his arms. "Your work seems very efficient, but I find it difficult to believe that we provided the exact amount you needed. What else can I help you with?"

The man scowls, clearly uncomfortable with the question. "We, uh, we are quite fine with everything you have already provided."

Ehren studies the man for a long moment before giving him a conceding nod. "Very well."

The man relaxes. "Is there anything else I can help you with, Your Majesty?"

I don't miss Ehren's barely concealed grimace at his title as he shakes his head. "No. I'm sure we will check in with you before we leave in the morning, but for now I think we'll relax and enjoy your town."

The man nods, launching into recommendations of how to spend our day. As Bram engages Melvin in conversation, Ehren pulls me aside.

"You think there are still parts of the town that need to be fixed, don't you?" I say before Ehren even gets a chance to speak.

"Yes, I do," he admits with a nod. "And I want you to help me dig. If there are any issues that still need funds, the villagers will know. Would you mind asking around?"

I nod. "I would be happy to, but am I the best choice?"

A smile plays on the corner of Ehren's lips. "Who should I send? Bram? His scowl will scare everyone away."

He mimics Bram with an over-exaggerated scowl. I choke on a laugh.

"You have a point."

"Good," he says, clapping a hand to my shoulder as he grins. "I knew I could count on you."

Ehren turns his attention back to Melvin as I sneak off as discretely as possible. I'm wearing my uniform, so there's no way I can blend in completely, but on my own I'm more likely to ease someone into casual conversation. I wander for a bit, pretending to be enraptured by the general scenery.

"You're part of Prince Ehren's Guard, aren't you?" a gentle voice asks from behind me.

I turn to find a young woman around my age eyeing me with interest. I suddenly wish I could turn on the charm I've seen many of the other Guards use on women. I do my best, offering her a smile. She brightens, so I must be doing it right.

"I am. My name's Cal."

"My name is Sadie," she says, inclining her head. She glances over her shoulder toward where Ehren still stands with Melvin and the other Guards. "Is the prince enjoying his stay?"

"He is," I reply with a nod. "He enjoys visiting villages around the kingdom. He truly cares for his people."

"It seems that way." She turns her full attention to me, tilting her head. "What about you? Do you like our village?"

"I do. It has a nice, homey feel to it. I grew up in Embervein, so I've always wondered what small town life was like. Do you enjoy living here?"

She nods. "It's quiet, so I suppose that's nice. I'd like to visit a big city like Embervein one day, though."

My mind is racing. What would Noah say in a conversation like this? How do you flirt with anyone, let alone someone you're not remotely interested in?

"Well, maybe one day you can come visit. I'd love to show you around."

Her eyes light up, and I feel guilty. I glance away, eager for a change of conversation.

"So, I guess the funds Prince Ehren supplied were enough to fix your village? It seems like everything is in good condition."

Sadie pauses before nodding slowly. "Yes, he was very generous."

"I don't suppose there's anywhere the money fell a bit short?" I look back at her, meeting her eyes, but she immediately glances away.

"He was very generous," she repeats.

"Sadie," I say, drawing her eyes back to mine. I offer her a gentle smile. "You can tell me."

She swallows, glancing around nervously, before leaning in and whispering, "Well, there is the mill."

"The mill?" I repeat. "What about the mill?"

"Well, we use the river to run the watermill to grind the wheat we grow. When the river flooded, it messed up the waterwheel. Most of the funds the prince sent went to repairing the town, and there wasn't quite enough left to repair the mill all the way." She pauses before adding quickly, "But we're very thankful for everything Prince Ehren provided."

"He knows how much you appreciate it. I swear he does. He'd never see you as being ungrateful," I say, offering her what I hope is a comforting smile.

She relaxes, reaching out to place her hand on my arm. I stiffen under her touch, but she doesn't seem to notice or care.

"I know that being on the road, traveling with the prince, probably means you haven't had a good meal in a few days. If you'd like you can—"

"Oh, I'm sorry, but if you'll excuse me I believe my captain is motioning for me to rejoin the group," I cut her off, looking over her shoulder toward Bram, who, thankfully, is looking my direction.

Sadie's face falls as she drops her hand. "Oh."

Fresh guilt swells through me.

"I'm sorry, Sadie, you seem like a nice girl . . ." I look back over at Bram. He really is motioning for me now. "I really do have to go. Maybe I'll see you later?"

Her nod lacks enthusiasm as I turn and quickly cross the distance to Bram.

"Did you find out anything?" Bram asks as I step to his side.

"Their watermill is still broken," I answer. "They need it to grind their wheat."

Bram nods once, storing the information. "Good job, Cal."

Bram steps away, leaning forward to whisper in Ehren's ear. Ehren's eyes brighten and he looks to me, shooting me a wink before turning back to Melvin.

"So, how much do you need to finish fixing your watermill?"

Melvin shrinks back, paling as something akin to fear flashes across his face. "I . . . Where did you . . . ? How . . . ?"

Ehren waves the man off. "It doesn't matter. What matters is that you need additional funds to restore your town. Shall we go somewhere more private and discuss the amounts you need?"

After a moment of hesitation, Melvin nods, leading Ehren away to talk without prying ears, Bram trailing behind. Their negotiations don't take long, and when Ehren returns he's glowing. His smile warms me. He really does love his people, and I love that about him.

We spend the rest of the day relaxing around the town. We enjoy a hearty lunch in the tavern followed by sweets from the local bakery. Once the village girls discover Ehren won't bite, they start flocking toward him, eyelashes fluttering. A few young men even join the crowd, eager to chat with the prince.

While Ehren draws most of the attention, many of the other Guards find pretty girls to flirt with. I stand off to the side watching, a little envious how easily they so openly show their affections and attractions without fear. The only other person who seems less than enthused by the girls is Bram, who scowls at every girl like she's the biggest security risk the kingdom has ever seen.

After a dinner of meat pies and ale, we divide up into the same rooms as the previous night. Once Ehren and I are alone, he turns to me, eyes shining.

"I need your help to sneak out," he says, grinning wildly.

My eyes widen. "What? No! Bram would kill me. And then he'd kill you."

Ehren waves me off. "Only if something bad happens, but it won't."

"You don't know that."

Ehren meets my eyes. "Please, Cal? I'll owe you."

I sigh and drop my shoulders. "I suspect you're meeting up for a secret tryst with someone you met in town today?"

Ehren's grin widens. "Yep."

I swallow my envy and groan as I concede. "Fine, but you have to be quick about it. We can't stay out all night."

"Well, I can't promise the quick part," Ehren says with a

roguish wink that makes my cheeks burn, "but I won't take *all* night."

My stomach twists with nerves as Ehren makes his plans to escape. We wait until everyone has officially settled down for the night and even Bram has retired to his room. I step out of the room and distract the guard outside the door while Ehren slips around him. I make an excuse to go downstairs and meet up with Ehren in the alley behind the tavern.

"You're the best, Cal," Ehren says, his sea-green eyes shining in the moonlight as he drapes his arm across my shoulders.

I shake my head, ducking out from under his arm. "Let's just get this over with so we can get you back in your room before Bram realizes you're missing and murders us both. Do you even know where to go?"

Ehren nods, licking his lips as he glances down the road. "Yes. I have directions."

"Then I guess it's up to you to lead the way."

Without missing a beat, Ehren sweeps into the streets, walking swiftly as he searches for the house he needs. He pauses, grinning, his hands on his hips, as he eyes a small two-story house on the edge of town with a single candle burning upstairs in a side window. He steps beneath the window and gives a low whistle. A head pops out, and my heart stills. It's not a girl, but a young man. I'm afraid we've been caught or have the wrong house, until a smile breaks across the face of the man in the window before he disappears back inside. I turn to Ehren, eyes wide and mouth gaping, sure I've misinterpreted something. The look of mischievous delight on Ehren's face tells me my initial assumption is correct.

"You . . . You're meeting a man?"

Ehren's face falls for a moment before he nods, watching me closely. "Yes. Is that a problem? Should I have mentioned it before?"

I'm still searching for words when a side door opens, the young man beckoning for Ehren to come inside. Ehren nods to the young man, glancing back at me, his expression etched with concern.

"Just wait outside. I won't be too long. We can discuss more later, if you like."

He disappears inside the house, and my stomach twists in knots. Ehren is with a man right now. I know for a fact he's been with women. I've known him for years and have seen him flirt, kiss, and meet up with women, but never a man. My head spins and my heart races.

I have no idea if Ehren's gone ten minutes or ten hours —I have no concept of time caught up in my swirling thoughts. When he finally reappears, he's ushered to the door by a half-dressed man, who leaves him with a parting kiss before shutting the door. Ehren's grin is wide and his eyes shining until his gaze falls on me. He straightens, a shadow crossing his face.

"We should get back," he says, brushing past me without even a sidelong glance.

I catch up with Ehren and we walk side-by-side in silence. I have a million questions but, for some reason, I can't find a way to voice them. Sneaking Ehren back inside proves to be easy, as the guard outside his door is asleep. I hope for his sake Bram doesn't find out. Once inside our room, Ehren turns to me.

"Well, are you going to ask?" His voice is far too tense.

I glance away, my chest tight. "I have no right to ask. It's not my place."

"You won't tell anyone, though? Not that I particularly care about people knowing, but it could complicate things if my father found out."

I meet his eyes. "Never. I'd never share your personal business with anyone." I pause before adding, "I just never suspected that you were interested in men."

Ehren relaxes, the bed creaking as he eases down on the edge.

"I don't necessarily have interest in men," he confesses, selecting his words carefully. "I have interest in . . . everybody, anybody. Men, women, people who don't ascribe to either—it doesn't matter. There are a myriad of things that attract me to different people and various aspects I enjoy during . . ."

He trails off, a grin twitching at his lips before he continues, his voice growing somber again.

"I'm sure I'll be forced into marriage with a woman one day, and when that day comes, I'll be fully and completely devoted to her. In the meantime, single nights here and there are meaningless. I'm not tempted to fall in love with any of them, and they keep me satisfied and distracted enough so I don't long for anyone who I might truly care for."

He meets and holds my gaze as I nod, my heart hammering so loudly I'm sure he can hear. Single nights. I wonder if . . . No. I push the thought from my mind. If I ever wanted to have any sort of relationship with Ehren, I want more than one night. I wouldn't risk our friendship over something so trivial, even if it would be like living a dream in many ways.

"Well, we should get some sleep," I say, tearing my gaze from his. I need this topic to be behind us before my mind can latch onto any more ideas or, worse, hope. "We have a long trip in the morning."

Ehren nods, his easy smile returning, though it doesn't reach his eyes. "You're right. Thanks for playing lookout. I owe you."

"You don't owe me anything," I counter, shaking my head. "You're my prince. I'm here to serve and assist you."

"But you answer to Bram."

"No, I answer to you." I look up and find him watching me in a way that makes me feel warm all over. I hold his gaze, unable to look away. "I'll always be here for you, Ehren, for whatever you need, whenever you need it."

Ehren's lips part as he studies me for a moment, head tilted in curiosity. It's almost as if he's searching for meaning behind my words, and I pray to the gods he doesn't detect the foolish emotions behind them. At length, he only nods.

"Thank you, Cal. You'll never know how much you— well, your loyalty, I mean—matters to me."

THREE

As much as I enjoyed our trip to Bellvale, I'm happy to be back in Embervein. I like the routine. At Bram's request, I continue observing soldiers who want to be part of Ehren's Guard. I try not to focus all my attention entirely on the young man with the hazel eyes and charming smile, but more often than not, he's the one I watch. He has fervor and determination that set him apart from all the other soldiers. Three days after we return from Bellvale, I finally learn his name—Makin Parelli. It fits him.

Every day after training, Makin goes and works by himself, practicing with a variety of weapons. When the next round of Guard trials arrives, he's there again, along with six other soldiers. This time, he makes it to the second round before failing. His failure is made even sharper by the fact two of the others complete all three tests. He trains even harder and longer the following week. I know because I watch him every day.

On the day before the next round of trials, I watch him train with daggers. His aim is fairly impressive, rarely missing the center of his targets. When he moves to another area of the training ring, his back blocks my view, so I move to a better position. It puts me closer to him, and I'm slightly more exposed, but he hasn't noticed me yet. He's on his third round of daggers when he speaks, his voice filling the empty air with warmth that sends chills down my spine.

"You know, I usually prefer to meet my stalkers in person, or at least know their names."

I freeze, my eyes locked on his back. He turns slowly, a wicked grin twisting on his lips as his eyes meet mine. I straighten, eyes wide with horror at being discovered.

"My guess is that you're not part of the prince's spy network," he teases, his eyes shining as he absentmindedly tosses a dagger spinning into the air, catching it flawlessly by the hilt. "If you are, then I'd say his spies need a bit more work."

"I'm not a spy," I manage, clearing my throat. "I'm a regular member of his Guard."

"I can see that," Makin says, nodding to Ehren's crest on my uniform.

"That's why I'm here," I say, my brain finally functioning again. "Captain Bramfield and Prince Ehren asked me to watch you. They have their eyes on you."

It's not entirely a lie. My words make his entire face light up, hope shining in his eyes.

"Really?" he asks, nearly breathless.

I nod, closing some of the distance between us. "They think you have potential."

Makin pauses, a shadow crossing his face as he eyes me warily. "This isn't a joke, is it? You're not making fun of me?"

I shake my head vigorously. "Not at all."

Makin's smile returns.

"But, you need some work if you're going to pass the tests, and that's only half the job. After that, you have to impress Captain Bramfield and Ehren on a more one-on-one basis."

"I know. I'm trying. You know I've been training twice as hard—you've been watching me—but I don't seem to be getting anywhere." He looks crestfallen, and I have to fight the urge to reach out and take his hand. His eyes light up as he looks into mine. "Can *you* help me?"

"What?" I ask, stumbling back a step.

He nods eagerly. "Yes, you're already a member of the Guard, which means you have the necessary skills. You know what they're looking for. You can help me."

I shake my head, glancing away. "I don't know that I'd be much help. I've never trained anyone before."

"Please? I really want this, but I can't do it alone. Surely while you've been observing me you've picked up on my weaknesses, the things I need to work on."

I meet his eyes and sigh. There's no way I can say no. Not to him.

"Fine. I'll help you."

Makin's face breaks out in a grin that stops my heart for a solid two beats, my breath catching in my throat.

"Thank you! You won't regret it. I swear." He pauses a moment before thrusting his hand toward me. "Name's Makin Parelli, by the way."

I don't bother telling him I already know his name. Instead, I smile and accept his hand.

"Callon Browen, but you can call me Cal."

"All right, Cal," Makin says, my name like honey on his lips. "Where do we start?"

"Well, your sword skills are good, but you concentrate

too much on attacking instead of responding to your opponent. You need to work on your defensive side and combine it with your offensive strategies."

Makin nods, absorbing my words. "Okay. Can we spar and you instruct me as we go?"

"Sure," I reply, struggling to hide a grin.

We spar for at least an hour. As we go, I correct little things about his stance and form. Things that are better than your average soldier, but still fall short of what Bram looks for in Guards. By the end, I can already see marked improvement. After swords, we practice a bit with a bow. I can tell immediately that Makin is strongest in this area and needs little work. When I tell him this fact, he brightens.

"My brother and I started bow hunting when I was almost too small to hold the bow," he says with a chuckle.

"You have a brother?"

Makin nods. "Yep. I have a brother a year older than me and a sister two years younger. What about you? Do you have any siblings?"

I shrug. "I don't know. Not that I know of, at least."

Makin stares at me, brow crumpled in confusion, so I explain.

"A midwife dropped me off at the Embervein orphanage when I was an infant. I know nothing about my family other than my mother died in childbirth. There was a small outbreak of sickness the year I was born that likely killed my father or any other family I might've had, but that's mostly speculation on my part."

"That's . . . sad."

I shrug again. "It is what it is. The orphanage was good to me, and I was taken care of. When I became a full soldier at age ten, I got to stay in the barracks."

"So, the Guard is your family?"

I look over at him, a smile playing on my lips at the thought. "I guess so, in a way."

"Well, that means when I get on the Guard with you, I'll be your brother."

He grins, but I have to work to hide my grimace. I don't want to think of him as my brother in the slightest. I force a smile.

"I suppose so. Anyway, I think we've trained enough for today."

"You'll train with me again tomorrow, right?" Makin asks. "I'm going to try to take the trials tomorrow, but I have a feeling I'll fail again. I need more practice. So, you'll help me again? Until I pass?"

I meet his eyes. "I'll be here for you as long as you need me."

He grins. "How about we celebrate our new alliance with a drink in the tavern? My treat."

"Sure. Why not?" I concede with a shy grin.

"Excellent! I think we're going to be great friends, Cal. You and I can take on the world and win. I just know it," Makin says, throwing his arm around my shoulders.

I hope he doesn't notice the red tipping my ears as I reply, "Oh, you're a Seer, now? Shouldn't you have included that in your introduction?"

Makin laughs. "Nah, I'm no Seer, but I'm good at judging people. You, Cal, are one of the good ones."

I'm still processing his words when we reach The Gilded Goblet. I hope he's right. I really could use a friend like him.

As PREDICTED, Makin fails the next round of testing, but he doesn't seem quite as upset. Instead, it seems to renew his enthusiasm. We meet for additional training every afternoon. He always gives his all, no matter how sore and tired he is from regular training. One day, he shows up particularly stiff. I try to convince him to take a day off, but he insists on training anyway. The next day, Bram and Ehren are busy with official business, and I get a chance to go watch Makin train with the other soldiers in lieu of my training. He's even more noticeably stiff and sore. I shake my head at his stubbornness. At least I know a way I can help him.

I leave the training field and head toward the healers' room in the castle. Inside, I find Healer Gwen wrapping a bandage around a maid's hand. Healer Gwen raises her eyes to me as I enter.

"I'll be with you in a moment," she says.

"You okay, Lola?" I ask the maid.

She meets my eyes and smiles softly. "I am. I just cut my hand on some broken glass."

"There," the healer says, securing the bandage. "You got lucky the cut wasn't too deep. Do be more careful."

Lola nods, her cheeks tinging pink. "I will." She looks up at me as she brushes past. "Bye, Cal."

I give her a parting nod before turning to Healer Gwen.

"What can I do for you?"

"I was wondering if you had any of that salve for sore muscles on hand?"

She nods and shuffles to her shelves of ointments and salves. "I do. Is Captain Bramfield overtraining you lads again?"

The bottles and jars clink together as she sifts through them.

I shake my head. "No, it's for a new soldier who's pushing himself a little hard."

"Ah! Here it is!" she says, carefully pulling a small jar from the back of a shelf. She walks over to me, holding it out. "You remember how it works, I presume? Rub it on the sore muscles and relief should come after a few minutes."

I nod, accepting the jar. "Yes, ma'am. Thank you."

I duck out of the healing room and head to the side training field to wait for Makin. When he arrives, he's moving slowly.

"You know, you really should take a break from these extra training sessions."

He grins. "And you know I'm not going to do that."

I roll my eyes but don't bother to hide my smile. "You're entirely too stubborn. That's why I got you this."

I toss him the jar of salve and he catches it with one hand. He lifts it, scowling at the label.

"A healing salve?"

I nod. "It's for muscle soreness. It's saved me on more than one occasion."

"Can you help me put it on?"

Makin tosses me the jar, but I fumble, nearly dropping it, distracted by Makin jerking his shirt over his head and exposing his bare chest. My heart pounds against my ribcage as I struggle to keep my breathing even.

"I, uh . . . Can't you do it yourself?" I stumble, trying not to ogle his muscular torso and failing miserably.

Makin raises his eyebrows. "I could, but it would be easier if you could help, me being stiff and all."

I take a shaky breath, my eyes dropping to the jar in my

hands. I swallow. I can do this. I draw another breath. This is a simple task. I should be able to do this.

"If it makes you uncomfortable, you don't have to."

I look up and find him watching with concern.

"I can do it," I say, but I can tell Makin isn't entirely convinced. "I can."

"Only if you're sure."

I force a smile. "Of course. Um, I'll start with your shoulders and then do your back."

Makin pauses, holding my gaze. "You're sure?"

I attempt a playful smile. "I wouldn't agree if I wasn't. Turn around."

Makin hesitates only for a moment before he turns his back to me. Without his eyes watching me I relax a little, but I still feel guilty admiring every bit of his body. I push my thoughts aside and focus on the task at hand.

I dip my fingers in the jar and inhale deeply. I can do this. I carefully rub the salve on Makin's shoulders. His skin is hot beneath my fingertips. He relaxes under my touch, rolling his shoulders so I feel the corded muscles moving. I press harder, working the muscles, and he releases a soft moan. I beg my body not to react as I continue, working my way down his back. Sweat beads on my brow and it has nothing to do with the heat from the sun. When I get to the base of his back, my heart is racing. I'm both relieved and disappointed to be done.

"Thank you," Makin says, turning to face me. "I can already feel it working."

I swallow, nodding as I place the lid back on the jar. "We should wait, though, before we practice. It takes a few minutes to be fully effective. You don't want to strain anything."

He nods, glancing around, his eyes settling on the low stone wall bordering the training ring. "Shall we take a seat then?"

I nod and follow him to the wall. He takes a seat and I settle next to him, making sure there are several inches between us.

"You should take the rest of this," I say, offering him the salve. "Put more on before bed and in the morning if you still feel stiff."

He takes the jar from my hand, his fingers brushing mine, and sets it next to him on the wall while an awkward silence sinks around us.

"You said you have a brother and a sister?" I say, tired of drowning in silence.

Makin nods, grinning. "Yep. Lilly and Oak."

"Oak? Like the tree?"

Makin laughs. "Yes, like the tree. I don't think he'll ever forgive my parents for naming him after a tree. It's the first thing everyone asks when they find out his name."

I chuckle. "I suppose that would get old fast."

Makin nods, thinking for a moment. "Want to hear a story?"

"Absolutely."

"Okay," Makin says clearing his throat. "Well, there's this old woman in my village. Well, she's not really that old, but old enough. Anyway, she's bitter and just all-around grumpy. She spends her days hating everyone and baking fruit pies that she sets to cool on her windowsill. One day, she got Oak in trouble with our parents over something—I don't even remember what—and Oak decided to get back at her by stealing one of her pies. She got so furious. She knew it was Oak, but we ate the pie before she could catch us with it. It was supposed to be a one-time thing, you know? But it was so much fun to make her mad, every time she baked a pie, we'd steal it."

My eyes go wide as I laugh. "You didn't!"

Makin's eyes gleam with mischief. "Oh, we most certainly did. We got away with stealing at least a dozen pies before she finally caught us. We got in so much trouble, but we had no regrets."

"Those pies must have been delicious." I laugh.

"Actually, they're the worst pies I've ever eaten. They were truly dreadful. We buried a few of them because we couldn't stomach to eat them." Makin grins, making me laugh even harder.

"Of course," Makin adds, "my sister is an amazing cook, so anyone's cooking compared to hers just falls short. She always knows exactly what to add to every recipe to make it one-of-a-kind. Have you ever had a cake with rose in it?"

I shake my head.

"Well, it tastes amazing, especially when paired with lavender tea. Lilly used to make it for me all the time."

Makin falls silent, a sad, thoughtful expression on his face.

"Do you miss your family?" I ask, my voice soft.

Makin nods, staring off. "I do. I miss them a lot, but I don't regret coming here." He looks over at me, meeting my eyes. "I've always wanted to be part of something bigger than myself. When I found out that Prince Ehren was forming his own Guard, I knew I had to try as hard as I could to join. I know I'm a simple soldier from a nothing village, but I still think I can make a difference."

"You *can* make a difference," I say, surprised by the fervor in my voice. "And you're more than a simple soldier.

I've grown up around soldiers my entire life and you're different. You have more determination than entire battalions combined. You're going to get on Ehren's Guard. I promise."

His eyes brighten. "Do you really think so?"

"I know so." I hold his gaze for a moment before forcing myself to look away. "Let's get back to training shall we? I'm sure we've waited long enough."

After our chat, Makin opens up more about his family. Every day, he shares another story until I feel like they're as much my family as his. I know about every birthday and holiday. I know their secrets and desires. But his stories don't pertain to his family alone. He starts to share stories about his friends from his hometown. His best friend, he tells me, has always been Oak, but he did make an exceptional effort to befriend another boy in his town by the name of Graham.

"I didn't care much for Graham as a person," Makin confesses as we practice throwing daggers at a target.

"Then why try to be his friend?"

Makin looks at me with a roguish grin. "Because Graham has a sister."

My heart sinks. All this time alone with Makin almost had me forgetting that most men prefer the company of women. Of course Makin is interested in women as well.

"Oh?" I manage.

"Yes. Her name was Cassie and she's the most beautiful creature I've ever seen. She had soft brown skin and bright, golden-brown eyes. Graham was incredibly protective of her, as you can imagine, and only his friends got close enough to even talk to her."

I focus on balancing a dagger in my hands to avoid looking at Makin. "So you became his friend?"

"Yep." He releases his dagger, hitting the target square in the center. "Bullseye!"

"Good throw."

"Thanks!" He reaches for another dagger. "Anyway, once I became friendly with Graham, I finally got to talk to Cassie."

Oh. Good. He didn't lose track of his conversation. Excellent.

"One day, we were all hanging out together when Graham had to leave for some reason or another. Everyone else left, but I stayed. Cassie and I finally got to talk alone. One thing led to another and we kissed."

Makin's eyes gleam with pride at his proclamation. I try to hide my shattered heart with a smile.

"Are you and Cassie still sweethearts?"

Makin shakes his head, plucking up another dagger. "Nah. I mean, I liked her, but we were never meant to be. I'm meant to be part of Prince Ehren's Guard, and she's meant to be the wife of someone else." His dagger flies through the air, just missing the center, but I feel like it's hit my heart.

FOUR

By the time the next round of trials arrives, Makin is much better prepared, but he's still extremely nervous. The morning of the tests comes after a full day of rain that left the training ground muddy and the air thick and muggy. The weather hasn't discouraged participants, however, and Makin is one of twelve soldiers vying for Guard positions. Ehren seems particularly enthusiastic about the odds.

"Surely one of them can pass," Ehren mutters to Bram. "Just one. That's all I'm asking."

"Makin has come a long way," I say, nodding to where he stands off to the side, his face schooled into careful concentration.

Bram looks sideways at me. "I heard you've been helping him train."

"A bit. He really has a lot of potential. He only needed a little guidance."

"Hm," Bram says, turning his attention back to Makin

and the other contestants. "It will be interesting to see how he has improved."

Since more participants than usual showed up, Bram decides to do the rounds differently, circling through each soldier and eliminating as they go before moving on to the next challenge. The first round is hand-to-hand combat, which is Makin's weakest, but he passes. Three others, however, don't make it to the next round. Round two is dagger throwing. Makin passes with flying colors, earning an impressed nod from Bram. Six more are cut. One of those cut demands another turn.

"I was close," he insists. "Give me one more shot. I can make it."

Bram shakes his head. "Try again next time."

I know this man. His name is Blake, and like me, he's been training as a soldier for Embervein since he was a child. Unfortunately for him, he lacks the natural talent and instinct to be more than a common foot soldier. Even if he did pass the tests, he would never make the Guard. Neither Bram nor Ehren can stand him.

"This is bullshit!" Blake yells. "This is all rigged!"

"Please, remove yourself from the field, or I will have you removed by force," Bram says evenly, clearly unfazed by Blake's outburst.

Blake holds Bram's gaze defiantly for a moment before he finally backs down. He's still cursing as he storms away. Bram clears his throat and steps to the center of the ring. He draws his sword and traces a circle in the mud. I scowl. As many times as I've watched the trials, I've never seen a challenge like this. Bram steps to the center of the circle and looks over at Makin and the two others that remain.

"For your final test," he says, his voice ringing through the air, "you will spar with me."

My heart sinks. Bram is by far one of the best swordsmen in the kingdom. Even the king's own soldiers and personal Guard won't go up against Bram.

"You won't need to disarm me, necessarily," he clarifies, and I breathe easier. "You will be timed for ten minutes. During that time, you must remain with me inside the circle. If you step outside the circle, you are disqualified. The same goes if you are disarmed or if I land a hit. However, if you can last the entire ten minutes, you pass. Any questions? No? Let's begin."

Bram motions to a lanky young man standing to Makin's right with dark eyes and ink-black hair. If I had to guess, he has some Northern Gleador heritage. Bram gives a nod to his time-keeper outside the ring, but I don't look away from the circle to see who it is. The contestant in the center ring is good at dodging. His footwork is quick, and he strikes fast and hard. He barely manages to hold his own, but he makes it to the end. He's breathing hard as he resumes his spot outside the circle, a wide grin on his face.

The next contestant is a younger soldier with bright red hair and freckles. He nearly makes it to the end, but steps outside the circle to dodge a blow from Bram. He leaves the circle crushed.

Makin steps into the circle next. He has a lopsided smile on his lips, but I can tell he's extremely nervous. The ten minutes begin and I watch every movement, afraid to even breathe. Makin moves like liquid, his footwork flawless. There are a few moments where he falls back on his previous training and nearly takes a blow, but he recovers quickly. He even makes several successful strikes against Bram. When the ten minutes is called, my mouth drops open. He did it. His eyes search and find mine in the crowd. I smile, giving him a thumbs up. He grins and turns his attention back to Bram.

The crowd begins to shuffle off, but Ehren and I hang back, stepping to the center of the ring where Bram is talking to Makin and the other man.

"Congratulations," Bram says. "You passed these tests, but that does not make you a part of the Guard yet. We need to make sure you are compatible with the current members and can handle the demands necessary. In order to test this, you will live and train with the Guard. Once we feel we have properly assessed your compatibility, you will receive our decision. Now, what are your names?"

"Nyco. Nyco Seong," the other man says.

Bram nods and turns to Makin, who straightens to attention.

"Makin Parelli, at your service."

"Well, welcome. I hope you both make it through, but if you do not, know you have already accomplished more than most."

Bram and Ehren leave and Nyco heads over to his group of friends. I approach Makin.

"Congratulations," I say, clapping a hand to his shoulder.

"I still can't believe it!" Makin grins. "This is literally a dream come true, and I owe you everything."

I shake my head. "You would have gotten here on your own."

"No, you helped me do this, and I'll never forget it. Let me show you my appreciation. I'll buy a round of drinks at The Gilded Goblet. What do you say?"

I look into his shining hazel eyes and know that I'll never be able to tell him no. I smile and nod.

"Sounds good. Then, after we've celebrated, we can get you moved into the Guard quarters."

Makin grins. "I can't wait to move in. Let's do that first."

I laugh at his enthusiasm but agree. We head straight to the barracks and Makin quickly gathers the few things he brought from home. The part of the barracks set aside for Ehren's Guard is larger and more open than the regular living quarters for other soldiers. We're divided up in rooms of two, and for a brief moment I regret that Noah's my roommate. We do find Makin a bunk a couple rooms down from mine, however, and I'm both thrilled and anxious to have him living so close.

Once Makin has unpacked his things and settled into his new room, we head into the city. The Gilded Goblet is rather full, but not overly crowded yet. I scan the room and spot Noah in the back corner with a couple other Guards. He sees me and waves us over.

"This is Makin," I say as we squeeze into the available spots. "He just passed the Guard trials."

"Hey! That's great!" Noah says. "Congratulations! Those challenges are no joke."

Makin grins. "Thanks! They were tough, but thankfully, I had help from Cal." Makin nudges me playfully and I grin over at him

Noah eyes me curiously, my grin vanishing. "So that's where you've been disappearing to. I was wondering. Thought maybe you'd found yourself a girl."

My blush deepens as I shake my head. "Bram and Ehren saw potential in Makin, too, so I just did what I could to help out."

I'm saved from any more conversation when the barmaid approaches the table. Makin and I place our orders before diving into the current discussion about an upcoming tournament. Makin fits in with the others so well, and I can't help but feel a little jealous—both at his ease of adapting and at sharing his attention. But he doesn't forget about me. Every couple minutes he glances over at me, and I have to fight to hide my grin. Makin is the only person who can make me feel seen in a sea of people.

"Well, what do we have here?" a voice slurs behind me.

I twist in my seat enough to see Blake hovering over my shoulder. I roll my eyes.

"It hasn't even been a day since this fellow passed his tests, and he's already sitting with the Guard like he's one of you," Blake says, clapping his hand on Makin's shoulder.

I noticeably tense, clenching my teeth. "What of it? He had the talent to get in, so why shouldn't he sit with us?"

"He's right," Noah says, coming to my defense. "He'll be one of us soon enough, even if only half of what Cal says is true."

Blake eyes me with a mixture of aggravation and amusement. "Maybe it's all about who you sleep with. Tell me, Cal, is that the case?"

My cheeks flush crimson, and it's suddenly very hard to breathe. I don't even dare look at Makin or any of the Guard at the table.

"I don't know what you're talking about," I mutter.

"Why are you asking Cal—" one of the other Guards starts to ask until Noah elbows him in the stomach, shushing him.

Blake's lips slip into a feral grin as he looks to Makin.

"You do know that Cal here doesn't go after girls, right? He only wants to be with men."

"How would you know?" Makin asks, his voice stiff but even. "Did you sleep with him? Or are you upset that he turned you away?"

Blake snarls, recoiling. "Hardly! As if I would debase myself in such a way. Noah told me."

I spin and look at Noah, my eyes widening with confusion. Noah looks at me apologetically, shrinking down in his seat. I shake my head.

"How . . . ? When . . . ?"

The man I thought my friend shrugs. "Every time we've been around women, you never flirt or go after them in any way. And I see the way you watch some of us when we're training and I just . . . I'm sorry."

I can't even look at Makin. I want to get out of here. My hands start shaking and I clench them under the table. Blake leans down, his face inches from mine. I squeeze my eyes shut, trying to block out the world.

"You're disgusting," he hisses. "If everyone on the Guard knew how disgusting you are, they'd probably want you dismissed. Maybe I should tell more people so I could have your spot. Let the news spread."

I feel a rush of movement at my side as Makin shoots to his feet. I open my eyes in time to see his fist connect with Blake's face. Everyone around us erupts into gasps and swears as Blake staggers back, his eyes wide as blood leaks from his now split lip.

"You don't get to come in here and call *my* friend disgusting. You're the only one here that's disgusting. Just because you lack the skills and talent to make it through the trials doesn't give you the right to attack those that do."

Blake's eyes flash as he wipes blood from his mouth with the back of his hand. "You're the one who attacked me."

"And I'll do it again if you don't move along."

Blake shakes his head, sneering down at me. "You can't tell me you're okay with—"

"I'm telling you right here, right now, along with anyone else who cares to listen"—Makin raises his voice so it carries across the entire tavern which has grown eerily quiet—"Cal is the best friend I've ever had besides my brother, and I am fine with him kissing or doing whatever he wants with whomever he wants. Not that it's any of my business. You need to leave."

Blake looks like he has a few more things to say but lifts his fingers to his lip and clearly thinks better of it, storming off through the crowd. Makin resumes his seat and glances over at me, but I can't bring myself to look up at him. I can't look at anyone. I want to disappear.

"Are you okay?" he asks, quietly enough I doubt anyone else heard him.

I shake my head.

"Do you want to leave?"

I nod.

Without a moment of hesitation, Makin stands, offering a winning smile to the others at the table.

"Well, it's been great meeting you all, but I think I need to head out. I still have some unpacking I need to do and Cal promised to help."

I stumble to my feet and follow Makin out of the tavern, focusing on the ground, too afraid to look at Noah as we leave. Neither Makin nor I say a word until we're out of the main part of the city, back on palace grounds. We go around to the side entrance that leads to the barracks, but I come to a halt several feet from the door. Makin stops in the doorway, turning to look at me.

"Do you want to stay outside for a bit?" Makin asks, watching me closely. "We don't have to go in yet if you don't want. We can stay out here and get some fresh air if you'd rather."

"Don't you even want to know if it's true?" I ask, my voice barely above a hoarse whisper.

Makin takes a step in my direction, his eyes locked on mine. "It doesn't matter to me if it's true or not. I meant every word I said. So what if you'd rather kiss boys than girls? What business is it of mine? It doesn't make you any less of a friend. I would be an idiot to let something as simple as who you love get in the way of our friendship."

My chin trembles as I struggle to hold back tears. "So, you really don't care?"

Makin shakes his head, closing the distance between us. "No, I don't care. Why? Does that Noah guy care?"

I glance away from Makin, shaking my head. "I . . . I don't know. I didn't even know he knew. I've never told anyone about . . . this."

I can't even say the words. They just won't form. I look back at Makin and a tear slides down my cheek.

"I never had a supportive family or anyone to tell me how these things work. I don't know if it's okay to feel this way. Everyone else seems to fall into normal relationships, at least publicly, so I don't have many examples to follow. I've tried to hide this part of me, but I guess there are some things you can't hide. It's who I am. I can't help what I feel."

"And that's okay, Cal. It's okay," Makin says, placing his hand on my arm. I involuntarily flinch at his touch and he drops his hand without drawing attention to the simple gesture. "No one else has the right to tell you how you can or can't feel. You got that?"

I nod, trying to force a smile. "Well, at least one positive thing that came from tonight is I finally got to see someone slug Blake."

Makin laughs. "Happy to assist. Let me know if you need me to deck anyone else for you."

My smile becomes more genuine. "I'll make a list."

"Now, I don't really need help unpacking, as you know, but we can still go hang out in my room for a bit if you want."

"You don't mind me being in your room?"

Makin shakes his head. "Not in the slightest. In fact, I don't seem to have a roommate, so if your current roommate does have any issues now that you're . . . out, feel free to take that spare bunk."

I nod and follow Makin inside. What *does* Noah think? How long has he known, and why didn't he say anything? I don't feel like getting the answers to my questions tonight, so I decide to stay closed off with Makin playing a game of cards until I know Noah will be asleep. I'll confront him another day. I've had enough confrontation for now.

FIVE

I'm up and out of the room the next morning before Noah wakes. My stomach is too twisted in anxious knots to bother with breakfast, so I head straight to a training field and run solitary sword drills. Sparring always relaxes me, helps me work through my thoughts, and gods know I have a lot of thoughts to sift through today. I'm starting to feel better when Noah approaches the field, undoing everything.

"That's some sharp sword work there," he says, nodding to my blade. "Care for a partner?"

I lower my sword and look Noah dead in the eye. "Not if that partner's you."

Noah's shoulders drop. "Look, Cal, I'm sorry I was partially the reason Blake found out, but—"

"Partially the reason?" I snap, my voice cold. "It sounds like you're the whole reason."

"I was talking with a few other soldiers and he was eavesdropping. I never meant for him to overhear."

"Why were you talking about me in the first place?"

"I wasn't talking about *you* exactly," he backtracks, avoiding my eyes. "The topic of men loving men came up, and I'd been drinking a bit. Your name slipped out. Entirely an accident. And I didn't say it was for sure true. I just mentioned that I suspected that you might..."

I storm past him, shaking my head. He catches my arm and I jerk around to face him. My expression must tell him I'm not to be messed with this morning because he shrinks away.

"You know what hurts the most about this, Noah?"

He shakes his head.

"It's that I thought you were my friend." I hate how my voice trembles as I say the words. I hate that it breaks on the word "friend."

Noah looks like I slapped him. "I—I am your friend, Cal."

"No," I spit. "Friends don't make assumptions and gossip behind each others' backs. If you wanted to know if I like men, then you should have asked."

"Would you have told me the truth?" he asks quietly, averting his eyes. "Because in all the years we've known each other, you've never mentioned it." He raises his gaze to mine. "We live together and you've never once hinted that you might be attracted to men. I think, if it's true, it's something you should have told me. It's not right that you hid it, sleeping feet away from me and all."

Now I feel like I'm the one who's been struck. I stumble back, shaking my head.

"Why? Do you think I would force myself on you in the middle of the night?"

"No! No! That's not what I—"

"Because, Noah, I hate to break it to you, but you are *not* my type. Even if you were, you have nothing to worry about because I'm better than that."

"Cal!"

"I don't want to talk about this anymore," I say, turning and walking away.

"Please, Cal, don't do this," Noah calls after me.

"I'll move out of our room so you won't have to worry anymore," I say without bothering to turn around. "Gods forbid you lose any sleep."

Noah calls my name a few more times, but I ignore him. Once I'm around the corner and well out of his sight, I start shaking uncontrollably as emotions overwhelm me. I sink down against an outer wall, my head in my hands. I inhale and exhale slowly, managing to eventually calm myself down. Once I have control, I go immediately to my room and gather my things. If Makin is surprised when I show up outside his room with all my stuff, he doesn't show it. Instead, he motions me inside and helps me set up my space. When we're done, we walk together to morning drills.

The next couple weeks fall into a comfortable pattern. Everything is essentially normal, except Makin is now by my side all day, every day. Noah tries to approach me twice, but a few threatening looks from Makin has him backing down, willing to give me my space.

Being around Makin all the time is like breathing clean, fresh air. I wake every morning light and happy and go to sleep feeling the same. In some ways, it's as if my life never really started until I met him, and he seems equally at ease with me. Even though he insisted he was fine with everything he learned about me, I keep expecting him to treat me differently, but he never does. He's still as friendly and caring as ever and every day I fall a little more in love with him.

He easily makes friends with the rest of the Guard, even falling into a good rhythm with Bram and Ehren, but there's still something special about how he interacts with me. He's warmer and more relaxed. I wonder if, just maybe, he feels the same about me as I do about him.

Almost exactly two weeks from the day Makin passed his test, Bram holds me back after morning drills.

"It seems Makin is acclimating well," he says, glancing past me to where Makin waits for me at the edge of the training field.

I grin and nod. "I think he'll make an excellent addition to the Guard."

"I'm inclined to agree, but I'm still a bit concerned by the fact that he's new to Embervein. Do you think he's loyal enough to Ehren?"

I nod without a hint of hesitation. "Most definitely. I will stake my life on the fact Makin is a needed member of the Guard."

Bram arches an eyebrow. "Your life?"

I nod. "My life."

"Very well, then."

Bram turns from me and motions for Makin to join us. When Makin reaches us, Bram extends his hand.

"Congratulations. You are welcome to join the Guard if you so desire."

Makin clasps Bram's hand, giving it a vigorous shake. "You mean it? You really mean it?"

Bram smiles and nods. "Yes. You have proven yourself sufficiently. You will have to swear your allegiance to Ehren to make it official, but otherwise you are a member of the

Guard. Cal can show you where you can get your uniform. Ehren is busy this morning, but we can arrange for you to swear an oath this evening. Is that acceptable?"

Makin's head bobs up and down eagerly. "Yes, of course!"

"Good. I wll leave you in the capable hands of Cal for now, and I will send for you this evening when Ehren is ready."

Bram strides off and Makin turns to me, his grin as wide as his face and his eyes shining brighter than stars.

"You did it," I say, matching his grin.

"Thanks to you," he replies, meeting my eyes.

Gods. I could get lost in those hazel eyes and be happy to never find my way home again. They are my home.

"You're the one that did all the work."

He shakes his head. "Don't even pretend you didn't have anything to do with it." His eyes still shine, but his expression grows somber as he adds, "I'm serious, Cal. You've been the best friend I could've asked for. I honestly felt a bit lost and out of place when I first arrived in Embervein, and your friendship made me feel accepted and welcome. You offered up your own time to a stranger, and I'm grateful for every bit of your help."

My cheeks grow warm as I duck my head. "It was nothing. I'm happy to help. Really."

Makin grins, throwing his arm across my shoulders as we turn to head off to morning duty. "Either way, I'm glad we found each other."

My thoughts are a swirl of emotions but I manage a soft, "Me too."

Our morning duty mostly entails walking the palace grounds, giving plenty of opportunity for other Guards to find and congratulate Makin on his new position. News is traveling quickly, it seems. Makin's floating on air the entire day, his grin hardly fading. The day is nearly over when a messenger finds us, telling us to meet Ehren in the throne room after dinner. Makin is all giddy nerves, barely eating a thing, so we leave dinner early to give him a chance to collect his thoughts and change into his new uniform.

My swearing-in ceremony for Ehren's Guard was a big deal because it was the first. It happened in the middle of the day and was attended by several nobles and other people of significance. Ehren wore his finest clothes, including his most formal crown. It was a very public event. Fifteen of us were sworn in that day. The next ceremony a few weeks later had less flash, but it was still attended by a fair amount of people. Only six were sworn in, Noah being one.

Since those first two, the ceremonies have been more simplistic and reserved. Makin's is no exception. Ehren wears a simple circlet crown, but nothing else looks out of the ordinary. He stands in front of the thrones, Bram by his side. As soon as we enter the room, he grins at us.

"Is Makin the only one being sworn in?" I ask, my eyes scanning the emptiness of the vast room.

Ehren shakes his head. "No."

Before he can tell me more, Nyco strolls in with two of his Guard friends. Ehren's grin widens. Nyco stumbles forward, inclining his head.

"Welcome," Ehren says. "I suppose we'll jump right in. Makin, Nyco, if you'll step forward, please."

Makin takes a deep breath, stepping from my side to stand directly in front of Ehren, Nyco to his left. Ehren's eyes shine as he meets Nyco's eyes and then Makin's, but his expression is somber.

"I hope you understand that being part of my Guard is a privilege as much as it is a duty. Your responsibility is to protect and serve. Loyalty is key, and should I ever doubt your loyalty, you will be dismissed immediately. While I am your prince, and while your duty will be to protect and serve me as I fulfill my duty to the crown and my kingdom, we are a brotherhood. We are a family made of bonds over blood."

Ehren locks eyes with Makin and Nyco in turn, letting his words sink in. Each nods before Ehren continues.

"If you proceed to swear an oath, you swear it to me and me alone. You are not swearing yourself to my father, though he is the king and his commands should be heeded. In return, I swear to you that I will forever put my kingdom and my people first. By serving me, you serve your kingdom."

Makin and Nyco nod again. Ehren's smile returns.

"Excellent," he says, drawing the golden sword sheathed at his right side in one smooth motion. "Kneel."

Without hesitation, Makin and Nyco drop to their knees, their faces lifted to Ehren. Bram steps forward, taking his place by Ehren's side.

"Makin Parelli, do you swear before these witnesses to honor and serve His Royal Highness Prince Ehren Andrewe Daniel Montavillier as he fulfills his duty to the Kingdom of Callenia?" Bram asks, his voice ringing through the throne room.

Makin bows his head. "I swear on my life."

Ehren steps forward and places his sword on Makin's right shoulder, crossing it to his left.

"I accept your oath and welcome you to my Guard."

Tears burn my eyes, pride swelling in my chest as I look at Makin. The process is repeated with Nyco, and then they are both asked to rise. Ehren grins at them, eyes bright.

"Welcome aboard, boys. We've got some adventures in our future. I can feel it. Now, who wants to join me for a celebratory drink?"

Ehren winks and I laugh while Bram sighs and rolls his eyes.

When we reach The Gilded Goblet nearly the entire Guard is present. Normally, I feel lost and alone in the crowd, but tonight I feel a part of something, like I belong. Makin glances at me every couple of minutes, and I find comforting warmth in his smile. I feel alive just being near him.

I get caught up in the celebration and drink tankard after tankard, quickly losing track of how many I've had. I rarely drink more than one or two, and since we left dinner early, it's all on a nearly empty stomach. I'm not sure if it's Makin's grin, Ehren's laugh, or the ale making me dizzy and light, but I don't care. I feel good. No, I feel amazing. I feel free. By the time we go to leave, I can barely stand. Makin laughs, catching me in his arms as I waver on unsteady legs.

"Careful!" He laughs.

I look up at him, grinning so wide my mouth hurts. His eyes shine as he looks down at me. This *must* be what true love feels like. I lean into him as he steadies me, looping his arm around my waist. He smells like sweat and grass and ale. He wraps his arm tighter as we stumble from the tavern and into the warm night air. He sings an off-key ballad I don't recognize as we stagger through the streets. When we reach the side door that leads to the barracks, Makin stops, releasing me and leaning against the wall of the castle.

"It's a beautiful night," he breathes, lifting his eyes to the stars shining above.

At least, I assume he's looking at the stars. I can't say for sure because I'm not looking at the sky. I'm looking at Makin, taking him all in. The way his throat moves as he swallows. His soft curls blowing in the night breeze. His bright, shining eyes. The precise curve of his lips. Gods. His lips. I wonder if they taste like ale. I wonder if they're as soft as they look.

I brace one hand on the wall behind him, tracing my fingers down his cheek with the other. His eyes meet mine, curious. My breath catches in my throat. I'm drowning in his eyes and I'll happily die here. I love him. I'm sure of it. Before I even realize what I'm doing, I'm pressing my lips to his. They're soft and warm, but they don't taste like ale. They taste like sunlight and salt.

Makin jolts away, his breath hitched as his eyes look at me in . . . horror? Oh gods. What have I done? I take a staggering step back, shaking my head, struggling to breathe as my heart pounds in my ears.

"I . . . I'm sorry," I mumble, the words like lead on my tongue. Gods. Why is the world spinning? I squeeze my eyes shut and press my palms against my eyelids. "I'm sorry."

"Cal," Makin says.

I shake my head harder, forcing my eyes open. I take several more steps back, and he doesn't try to cross the distance. Why would he? He's probably afraid I'll assault him again. He's practically dissolving into the wall, staying as far away from me as possible. Gods, I'm an idiot.

"I'm sorry," I say one last time before I turn and run.

Running in the dark when you're incredibly drunk isn't easy, but my shame drives me. I have to get away. I have no idea how I'll face Makin again. I can't face him again. I stumble to a stop, looking around to gather my bearings. I'm not sure if it's the ale in my system or the tears clouding my vision, but I only have a vague awareness of my surroundings. I feel so lost. I crumple to the ground, putting my head in my hands. I'm such an idiot. I've messed everything up. The tears come faster and harder, shaking my whole body. I can't control them, and I don't think I want to.

"Cal?"

I jerk my head up. Ehren stands above me, looking down, face etched in concern. He drops to his knees in front of me.

"What's wrong?" His voice is so kind, so gentle. So much more than I deserve.

"I'm an idiot. That's what's wrong. I've messed everything up. I can't even go back to my room," I ramble, my words slurring together so much I wonder if Ehren can even make sense of them. "I'll have to sleep out here tonight. At least it's warm."

"No," Ehren says firmly. "You're coming with me."

I shake my head and half-scoot, half-fall away from Ehren. "I can't go in there. I can't face him. Please don't make me."

"Who?"

I shake my head, covering my face with my hands. "It doesn't matter. I can't see him. I messed up. I messed up so badly."

Ehren wraps his arm around my waist and hoists me to my feet.

"Well," he says, leading me forward, "I have no idea what you think you did or what you're talking about, but I'm not leaving you out here."

"You can't take me to the barracks," I plead, struggling to get out of his grasp to no avail.

"I'm not," Ehren replies, tightening his hold on me. "I'm taking you to my room."

My face grows hot, and I look over at him. "Your room? But . . ." Suddenly the world tilts and everything feels very wrong. "Ehren, you need to let me go."

"I told you—" he starts, but he doesn't get a chance to finish.

Everything I had to drink comes up, covering us both in sick. Ehren releases me and I stumble back in horror. I cover my mouth, but it doesn't stop more from rising up, splashing over my shoes. I've never felt so ashamed. This is literally the worst night of my life.

"I guess this means we're changing and taking a bath before bed."

Ehren reaches toward me and I jerk back. "What are you doing?"

"I'm taking you inside and cleaning you up."

I shake my head. "You can't do that. You're the prince."

He flashes me a smile. "Exactly. I'm the prince, so I can do whatever I want. Luckily for you, I want to make sure you're properly cared for. Let's go."

I'm still shaking my head as he slips his arm around me, guiding me back toward the castle. I'm tired and dizzy, so I barely register any of our movements as we head to his room. Once inside, he kicks off his boots and immediately begins stripping out of his clothes. I stand, mouth gaping as I stare at him. He's all lean muscles, soft and sharp edges side-by-side in perfection, shaped by years of training. When he starts slipping his pants off, I manage enough cognizance to turn away.

"Please, I can't do this," I mumble. "I . . ."

"Sorry, I forgot this makes you uncomfortable," Ehren replies. "I'll go in the dressing room, but you need to change, too. I'll get you clothes."

I wait until I know for sure he's gone before I undress. My Guard uniform is revolting and I almost start retching again at the sight of it. I feel very exposed, standing nearly naked in Ehren's room. When he returns he carefully averts his eyes.

"I laid a change of clothes next to the tub. It's filling now."

I frown at him in confusion. "What?"

"You need to wash," he insists, nodding at the mess of clothes at my feet. "I'll send that off to be cleaned."

"You need to bathe first."

"I'll wash up when you're done."

"But—"

"Cal, consider it an order. Go take a bath before the water gets cold."

Without another word I stumble into his washroom. The water is just warm enough that it almost lulls me to sleep. I shake my head, splashing water on my face. I need to hurry. Ehren needs a bath, too. I trip out of the tub and slip on the pants Ehren laid out nearby, followed by a loose cotton shirt. My head pounds a loud, steady rhythm as I leave the washroom. I find Ehren lounging on one of the couches, reading.

"It's all yours," I mumble, shame coloring my cheeks.

Ehren nods, standing and striding toward me. He stops a couple feet away and meets my eyes.

"Do you want to talk about it? Whatever it is that has you so upset?"

I shake my head and glance down.

"All right. If you ever change your mind, I'm here." I nod, still not looking up. "Pick a couch and make yourself comfortable. If you need anything else, just ask."

He starts to move past me but stops, placing a warm hand on my damp shoulder.

"I mean it, Cal," he whispers. "I'm here if you need to talk. I'll always be here for you."

I give him one sharp nod before he drops his hand and disappears into the washroom. Tears of disgrace burning my eyes, I cross the room and settle on a couch. I feel like an intruder, but I'm far too drunk to think of a better solution. Instead, I sink into the throes of sleep, praying that I'll wake up to find tonight was nothing more than a horrible nightmare.

SIX

When I wake the next morning, it takes me a moment to remember where I am. Even after I realize that I'm in Ehren's room, it takes another few minutes to remember why. My pounding head is a reminder. I bury my face in my hands, shame twisting in my gut.

"How are you feeling this morning?"

I yank my hands down and look up as Ehren strides into the room. My stomach swirls with fresh humiliation and guilt. Oh, gods. I think I'm going to be sick again.

"I already requested some coffee and breakfast," Ehren says casually, like he's used to finding hungover Guards in his room every morning. Hell, maybe he is. "It should be up in a minute."

"Ehren, I . . ."

I don't even know what to say. There's too much to be said and not any words that fit the way I need them to. I need to thank him for his help. I need to apologize. I need to make sure everything is still okay between us.

Ehren's eyes meet mine and he offers a small, tight smile. "Do you remember last night?"

I glance away, unable to hold his gaze. "Enough."

"Do you want to talk about it this morning? It's fine if you don't."

I look back up at him, shaking my head. "No. I want to forget everything about last night."

"It's your choice," Ehren replies, stepping closer. "If you decide you need to talk it out, I'm available. I'll always make time for you and that's a promise."

I'm saved a response by a servant knocking with breakfast.

"Food. Excellent," Ehren grins, dropping down at the table. He glances back over to me. "Well, aren't you going to join me?"

I still feel unsteady as I rise, taking the chair next to him. He pours a cup of coffee and slides it to me before reaching for a second cup to fill for himself. I almost smile as I accept the cup and take a gulp of the bitter liquid. Neither of us speak as we eat from the selection of sausages, eggs, and fruit sent up by the kitchen. Well, Ehren eats. I can't stomach more than a bite or two, but the coffee does help clear my head. Ehren is finishing off the last bits of his breakfast when there's a knock on the door.

"Come in," Ehren calls.

The door swings open and Bram strides in, a Guard uniform draped over his arm. His eyes fall on me and his forehead knits in confusion. I avert my eyes.

"Morning," Ehren greets Bram cheerfully and a little too loudly.

"Good morning," Bram replies. "I brought the uniform

you requested. I wondered why you needed one, but I assume it is for Cal?"

I raise my eyes to Ehren's, my lips parting in confusion. Why is he helping me? Not that any of this is out of character for him—he's always been kind and thoughtful. I simply don't know that I'm deserving of his assistance. I'm the one that screwed up, and Ehren had no part in it. And yet, he's going out of his way to make everything easier on me, without caring how any of this could reflect negatively on him.

Ehren smiles, taking a sip of his coffee as he nods. "Indeed it is."

Bram holds the uniform out to me. I stand, accepting it in a haze.

"Do I even want to know what's going on?" Bram asks, his voice flat and his eyes darting from me to Ehren.

Ehren flashes Bram a wide grin and a wink as I flush a deep crimson from the tip of my ears all the way down my neck.

"Nothing. Nothing happened—is happening," I fumble, shaking my head. "I . . . Last night . . ."

"Cal celebrated a bit too much last night and crashed here to recover," Ehren says with a wave of his hand.

Bram releases what I assume is a sigh of relief.

"Can I use your dressing room?" I mumble, staring down at the uniform in my hands.

"Of course, Cal," Ehren replies. "If you need anything else, let me know."

I race to the dressing room, happy to close the door behind me. I dress quickly, my thoughts tumbling together in a blur. As much as I don't understand it, I'm grateful for Ehren's help. He's making this horrible situation a little better, even if I'm mortified he witnessed me at my worst. And everything with Ehren doesn't even hold a candle with everything I did wrong involving Makin. There's no way I can face him. Not yet. Possibly not ever.

When I reenter the main room, I'm happy to find Bram still present.

"Captain Bramfield," I say, using the most confident voice I can.

Bram looks to me, arching an eyebrow at the use of his formal title in a casual setting. "Yes?"

"Would it be possible for me to take up night duty instead of my usual morning rounds?"

Bram considers me for a moment before slowly nodding. "I suppose that can be arranged. You need more time to recover from last night?"

"I'd like it to be a permanent change, if possible."

Bram frowns and Ehren twists in his chair to look up at me.

"What? Why?" Ehren asks, his voice laced more with concern than curiosity.

I don't look down at Ehren, keeping my eyes locked on Bram. "I need a change of pace."

"I will see what I can do," Bram says after another moment of thought.

"Thank you," I reply, inclining my head. "Now, I suppose it's time for morning drills?"

"Do you feel up to that?"

No. Not at all. My head is pounding and I could hurl at any moment. But if I don't power through this morning I'm not sure I can manage future mornings. I need routine. I need to force myself to move forward or I'll fall.

"Yes, I can manage."

"Cal," Ehren says, rising from his chair. I still can't bring myself to look directly at him. "If you need time, you're welcome to stay here with me. I don't have anything I need to do this morning, so my plans are to stay in my room and read. I don't mind if you—"

I shake my head, cutting him off. "I'm fine. I need to get back into things. Back to routine."

Ehren looks unconvinced but nods. "All right. If you change your mind, I'll be here."

"Thank you, but I'll manage," I say, finally shifting my gaze to Ehren and offering him a tight smile.

"Well, then, we should be on our way or we will be late," Bram says, turning toward the door.

We walk together to morning drills in blessed silence. I half expect to be the source of morning gossip, sure everyone knows by now what a disaster I am, but no one is acting any differently than usual. That is, until Makin arrives. He has dark circles under his eyes and his hair is tousled and messy. I wonder if he got any sleep last night. When he sees me, his eyes widen and he heads my way. I immediately turn away, happy that drills are starting. When the morning training session ends, I put as much distance between myself and Makin as possible. Bram pulls aside one of the other Guards and assigns him to Makin for morning rounds. I can feel Makin's eyes boring into my back as I purposefully ignore him. He already hates me. He has to. I'm sure he's probably relieved to have someone else assigned to him.

The next few days fall into a simple, basic pattern. I spend my nights on duty, roaming the outside of the castle in peace. The morning drills are the most difficult time to avoid Makin. I have to arrive almost late and leave immediately. After drills, he goes with his new partner, and I sneak back to our room to get a few hours of sleep. Sometimes I avoid our room altogether, finding random corners and crevices to curl up in. I skip most meals and, when I do attend, I only stay long enough to shove a few bites of food in my mouth. I'm not hungry anyway. Food only turns my stomach.

Tonight marks one week since I screwed everything up. I slink into the dining hall several minutes after dinner has started, taking a seat at the far end of the table. I feel Makin's eyes on me the entire time, and it takes every ounce of self-control I possess not to look at him. The food tastes like ash in my mouth, and it's all I can do to swallow. I manage only a couple bites before I push back from the table, eager for fresh air. I head directly to one of the side training rings, taking out my sword. I feel light-headed from the lack of food and sleep, but it doesn't stop me from swinging with all my might. Anger and frustration well up inside me as tears burn my eyes, a few breaking free. I swing harder as more tears come.

"Cal," a soft voice says from behind me.

I spin and see the silhouette of a man in the shadows. Ehren steps forward into the silver moonlight, his eyes fixed on me. My shoulders drop and I turn my back to him.

"Don't worry. I'll be on time for night duty."

"Cal, I'm not worried about that at all. In fact, I order you to take the night off," Ehren says, his voice firm but gentle as he approaches.

I spin to face him, shaking my head. "No. I can't. I have to be on night duty."

"Why?" Ehren asks, searching my face. "What happened?"

I shake my head. "Nothing."

"Callon Browen, you tell me right now what has you so upset that you aren't eating or sleeping or taking care of yourself."

I clench my teeth, my eyes flashing as they meet Ehren's. "Is that an order?"

"Yes," Ehren says. Then, he takes a shaky breath, raking his hand through his hair as he looks away. "No. It's not an order." He brings his gaze back to me, and I can see the depths of concern reflecting in the sea-green pools of his eyes. "But please tell me. It pains me to see you like this."

I swallow and glance away, shaking my head as more tears break free. "I can't."

Ehren reaches out and places a hand on my arm. "Please, Cal. I can't take seeing you like this. It physically hurts me to see you suffering. I know there's a social divide between us —I'm a prince and you're a Guard, but you're *my* Guard. One of my first. We've trained together. We're . . . we're friends. Remember?"

I raise my eyes to his, releasing a shaky breath. "Yes, we're friends. But, Ehren—"

"Then, please, confide in me," Ehren cuts me off as he tightens his grip on my arm, his eyes boring into mine, his voice edged with desperation. "I want to help you. Please let me."

I'm suddenly very aware of how close he stands, barely a breath away. I step back, pulling from his grasp. My chest feels tight and my gut twists as I weigh my options. Telling him the truth could change everything, destroy everything. Not that I exactly have everything together now.

"Please, Cal," he whispers again, his voice breaking as he says my name.

I cover my face with my hands, shaking my head as I stumble back another step. "You'll think differently of me."

"I won't," he says, his voice filled with fervor as he steps toward me, taking my hands in his and pulling them from my face to look into my eyes. "I swear on my life."

My heart pounds so hard I feel like it could break free at any moment. Maybe he will understand. He, of all people, may understand. He's attracted to men, too. But, then again, he also sleeps with women. It's different. We're not the same.

"Please," he says, choking on the word. It's only then I realize he's on the verge of crying. "Please, Cal. I'm begging you. *Please.*"

I nod, looking down at my hands, still in his. I take a rallying breath and whisper, "I'm attracted to men."

It's the first time I've said the words out loud. The first time I've actually told someone. Even when I was accused before, I never actually said the words. I simply didn't deny anything. I raise my eyes back to Ehren, lifting my chin.

"I'm attracted to men," I say again, this time with more confidence. "And I have no interest whatsoever in women."

Ehren's face is a sea of conflicting emotions I can't sort through. His grip on my hands tightens for a fraction of a second as his eyes lock on mine. He licks his lips and glances away. My heart races faster with every second he stays silent.

"You know that I . . ." He pauses, shifting his gaze back to me. "You were there. You know about me. Did you think I wouldn't accept you? Why would you be afraid this would change anything?"

"Because it's different for you," I say, the words tumbling out. "You still flirt and dance with women. You steal kisses and cast furtive glances, so even if people knew, they wouldn't care. In the end, they know you'll settle down with a woman and produce heirs and be . . . normal. I'll never be like that."

Ehren laughs bitterly and shakes his head, finally releasing my hands. They feel cold without his warmth.

"You're right," he says, his voice thick. "I probably will marry a woman and produce heirs, like the good little prince I have to be, but it doesn't mean I haven't—can't—fall in love with a man."

He hesitates, as if he's debating his next words. When he speaks, it's with renewed determination, his hands clenched in tight fists at his side. "If I would let myself, that is. But I'll never let myself fall in love. I can't. I won't."

He glances away, something about him broken—something I have the sudden desire to mend. My heart clenches. I start to reach out to take his hand, but I pull back before he can notice.

"Why?" I manage.

Ehren looks up at me, his eyes meeting mine with such an intensity it's like looking directly into the sun. "Because the chance I will get to choose whom I marry is slim. My father will undoubtedly select my future bride, regardless of my desires, with little to no input from me. So, for me, the occasional secret rendezvous in the middle of the night is the only chance I have to be who I am. If I were to actually allow myself to love someone, only to be forced to let them go, to break his—their—heart . . ." He sighs and shakes his head. "It doesn't matter. I've made my peace with it. And I don't care if you only like men. It doesn't change who you are." He pauses. "Do you know why I wanted you on my Guard?"

"I assume it was because I've got the necessary skill."

Ehren smiles, his eyes brightening. "That much is true, but it was more than that. I had my eye on you for years."

"What?" I ask, breathless.

Ehren's smile grows as he nods. "You're loyal, brave, kind, caring, and everything I wanted in my Guard. I knew it from the first time we trained together as boys, even though I hadn't really started planning my Guard then. I still recognized all your amazing attributes and knew I wanted you by my side. You are an amazing person, Cal, in every way. Your loving men isn't going to change any of that. It's part of who you are as much now as it was when I first met you. It adds to all the things that make you . . . you. If someone can't see that, if they can't accept you—"

He stops, his smile fading as his eyes go wide, something lethal flashing across his face. "Is that what happened? Did Makin—"

"No," I rush, my tone defensive.

"Cal, did Makin say something or do something?" Ehren presses, his jaw set. "Even Bram is concerned about some fallout between you two, which means it has to be obvious as hell."

"No," I say firmly. "Makin is accepting. He's even defended me against others. I just . . . I screwed up, Ehren. I . . ."

A fresh tear slides down my face as the pain of everything rears up fresh. Ehren's hand moves from his side and, for a brief moment, I think he's going to reach out to me and take my hands again or pull me into his arms. But his hand freezes midway between us, clenching into a fist as it falls. He grits his teeth, his fist opening as he flexes his fingers at his side. Time is lost as I stare into his eyes, struggling to decipher what he's thinking. He licks his lips and shifts closer, holding my gaze. We're barely an inch apart now. My heartbeat quickens as my breathing becomes increasingly unsteady.

"Cal, I . . ." He stops short as his eyes focus just past me, an expression close to resignation settling on his features as he takes a wide step back. "You don't have to tell me, but I think you should talk to Makin."

"I can't. He probably hates me."

"I highly doubt that's true."

"How can you know?"

"Because," Ehren says, looking back into my eyes as a tight smile forms on his lips, "he's standing over there, looking very concerned."

I turn so fast I nearly topple over. Sure enough, several yards away, Makin watches us. My heart skips a beat as Ehren steps up next to me.

"I don't know what happened," Ehren says slowly, shoving his hands in his pockets. "But if you can work it out, you should try. If you need me, I'll be in my room. I'm here for you, Cal. Always. I mean that."

I manage a weak smile. "Thanks."

"Now," Ehren says, giving me a nudge with his shoulder, "go talk to Makin. Discuss everything that needs to be discussed, and then you go get something to eat. Don't think I haven't noticed you avoiding meals. I need my Guard strong and able."

I offer Ehren the first genuine smile I've managed in days. "All right."

He turns and saunters away, shooting me a wink over his shoulder before he fades into the darkness. I stay put, breathing in and out slowly in an attempt to steady my racing heart. When I turn around, I start, discovering Makin mere feet away. I don't even realize he's crying until he speaks.

"I'm so sorry," he says, his voice shaking. "I messed up, I think, and I don't know how to fix this."

I stare at him in bewilderment, processing his words. I take a step toward him as he continues.

"I didn't react well, I know that. I wasn't expecting it, though maybe I should've been. I'm sorry if I led you on. I didn't mean to."

"Makin," I say, taking another step toward him, but he cuts me off shaking his head.

"No, I'm sorry. I messed everything up. You're the best friend I've ever had, other than Oak. These last few days without you have been miserable. I want my friend back, but I don't know how to accomplish that."

I close the distance between us, tears on my cheeks. "Makin, you didn't do anything wrong."

"I must have!" he insists, his voice echoing through the night.

I shake my head. "How can you think any of what happened is your fault?"

He furrows his brow in confusion. "I must have done something to lead you on and then I rejected you."

"Makin," I say, struggling to keep my voice steady, "are you attracted to men in the the slightest?"

Makin pauses, his eyes meeting mine before he shakes his head. "No," he whispers, his voice barely audible. "No, and trust me, I've thought about it *a lot* this past week. Considered every option, but no, I'm not. I love you like a brother, but I can't love you like you love me. I'm sorry. I really am."

His confession feels like a dagger to my heart, but it's not unexpected. I exhale slowly.

"You are not responsible for any misinterpretation on my part. I read into things." I pause, glancing away. "Can you accept the fact that I do want men? That I may be in love with you and that my feelings may never change?"

Makin nods. "Yes. I don't care who you love or who you want to be with. I can't promise to ever return your affection, but I will never think less of you for it. I will stand by your side until the end. If you'll let me, that is." He pauses, something close to fear flashing across his features as he whispers, "*Will* you let me?"

I search his face. Can I continue a friendship with the man I'm in love with, knowing it will never be reciprocated like I want? Knowing that one day he'll find a nice girl and settle down to have a family? I smile softly, the answer coming to me instantly. Yes. Because a piece of Makin is better than no Makin at all. Maybe one day I'll even be able to move on, find someone who loves me as much as I love him. For now, however, I think I can handle whatever relationship Makin allows.

"I don't want to live my life without you," I admit. "So, as long as you're okay with me being who I am, if you can accept me and how I feel about you, then, yes."

Makin's shoulders sag with relief. "Thank the gods."

He throws his arms around me in a full embrace and I flinch. He jerks back.

"I'm sorry," he says, quickly.

I laugh. "You're fine. I just wasn't expecting it."

Makin grins. It's lopsided but perfect. He throws his arms around me again, and this time I lean into his embrace. When he pulls back his eyes are shining.

"So, do you think Bram will let you off night duty?"

"I think he will. At least, I hope so."

Makin drapes his arm over my shoulder and guides me toward the castle. "Well, let's go find him and fix everything. As much as I've enjoyed taking rounds with Jasper, I rather prefer your company."

I chuckle, glancing over at him. "Thank you. For everything."

Makin returns my grin. "Of course. Though, I hope you know this means you're stuck with me now. For always. You're never getting rid of me."

I laugh. "I'm counting on it. You and me, Makin. Together for always."

ALWAYS DOESN'T NECESSARILY MEAN FOREVER. I know that now. I know it because I'm still breathing. My heart still beats inside my chest. I know, because with every pulse, it hurts more. I'm still alive by some cruel twist of fate, but Makin is buried beneath the mound of loose dirt at my feet.

My chest constricts and I struggle to breathe. Tears burn my eyes, but I'm tired of crying. I'm not even sure how I'm still producing tears at this point.

I drop to my knees, unable to find the energy to stay standing. I feel a hand on my shoulder and I look up into a pair of bright green eyes. Alak gives my shoulder a slight squeeze as Astra drops down next to me, resting her head on my other shoulder. I'm vaguely aware of Bram standing behind me as Nyco steps next to Alak. Even Sama joins me at the graveside. Only one person is missing—one very important person.

Ehren's absence gnaws at what remains of my heart. Not only because I want him here, longing for the comfort only he can provide, but because I know what his absence likely means. Makin died saving me. Ehren is short a Guard because of me. I only hope he can find a way to forgive me, because living with Ehren hating me is worse somehow than outliving Makin. I don't want to navigate this world alone. I need Ehren.

Astra shifts, taking my hand, and I lean my head against hers. I guess I'm not alone. Not really. But I still somehow feel lonely. Emptiness is hard to fill when the person you love doesn't love you back. Maybe I'm star-crossed, forever destined to be alone. Something tells me if I hold on a little longer, I will find a way to fill the hole in my heart. I just need to trust that Fate has a plan and maybe it's even better than anything I could ever hope for or accomplish on my own. That's worth making it to tomorrow—the hope that one day everything will be good again, and I can find some version of a happily ever after.

Acknowledgments

So much of this book was me. It was a book of self-discovery. Through it I gained a lot of confidence in myself. And I am happy to share those little pieces with you.

Along the way I received a lot of support from a great group of people. So thanks to Lana for reading those early drafts that barely made sense. I owe you one. And Megan, Shanti, and Karin, your input was also greatly appreciated.

I also have to say a special thanks to my partner who put up with all my ramblings. I also made them read those early drafts that really should be considered a crime. But they were patient and kind and not only listened to my rambling and read my book, but also provided some great art for me.

Also thanks to Andi, my editor, for catching all those random commas. I still can't be convinced that commas have rules, but she knows better. She took a rough book and made it shiny.

And last but certainly not least, thank you, Reader. It is for you I write and I'm glad you returned for this novella. I hope we meet again soon.

About the Author

Amber D. Lewis is a new adult fantasy author with a Bachelor's Degree in Publishing. She currently lives in Taylors, SC with her partner and three kids. When she's not reading or writing books, you'll probably find her wandering the aisles of Target.

The Fire and Starlight Saga is Amber's first series, though she plans to write many more.

facebook.com/amberdlewisofficialauthorpage

instagram.com/mugshots_n_bookthoughts

bookbub.com/profile/amber-d-lewis

www.ingramcontent.com/pod-product-compliance
Lightning Source LLC
Chambersburg PA
CBHW021748190726
48290CB00008B/2537